My Dads

Kelly Bennett

illustrated by Paul Meisel

WALKER BOOKS
AND SUBSIDIARIES

LONDON · BOSTON · SYDNEY · AUCKLAND

I have two fathers.

I call this one Dad,

and this one Pa.

To meet them, you'd think Dad and Pa were as different as two fathers could be.

Pa is bald.

Dad is not.

Dad is tall.

Pa is not.

Pa wears boots.

Dad wears suits.

Pa takes pictures.

Dad takes naps.

Dad's into gadgets.

Pa's into plants.

Dad likes to fish.

Pa *is* a fish.

Dad and I
play sports.

Pa and I
play games.

Pa and I swap stories.

Dad and I swap jokes.

Dad teaches me to cook.

So does Pa.

Pa teaches me to paint.

So does Dad.

Dad loves
music.

So does Pa.

Pa loves biking.

So does Dad.

They both help me.

They both cheer me.

In some ways Dad and Pa
are as different as can be.
But in the most important way
they are exactly the same –

they both

Dad and me.

GLUE STICK

MUSEUM
ADMIT ONE
ADMIT ONE

ove me!

SEEDS

Pa and me.